Winnie & Maren,

Hope you enjoy the
Adventures of Solda &
can find all the lizards
hidden in the pages.

Enjoy!

M &
Solda.

Golda has brought joy to many as she has spent her life traveling North America. It is my hope that she brings joy to many more through the Adventures of Golda series.

For Emma Grace

R. Kinney with snuggles from Golda the Adventure Dog

A smile warms the heart. The sound of a giggle, a little finger finding a hidden treasure, and just bringing delight to a young face is my motivation as an illustrator. In some small way, may Golda's adventures be a place of joy, a place to dream and a place of discovery. Please share a smile and enjoy the simple riches that warm your heart!

In Joy and Light, Noryce with Twizzler

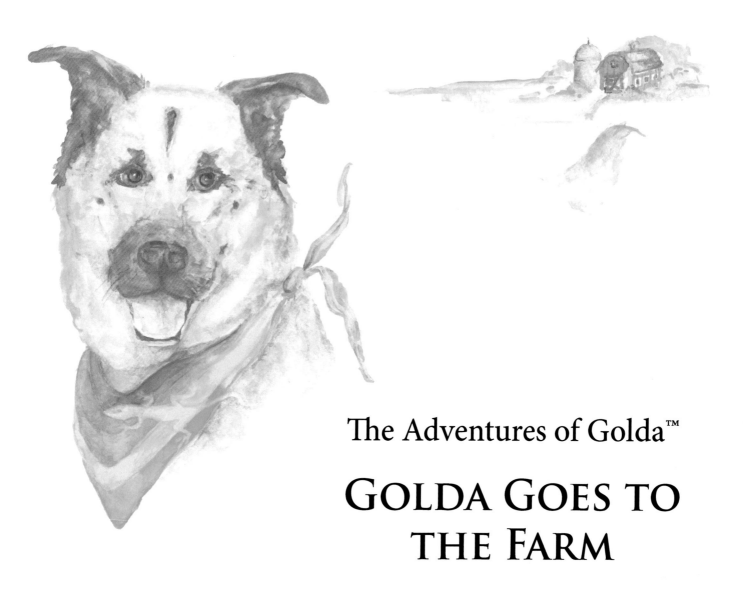

The Adventures of Golda™

GOLDA GOES TO THE FARM

R. Kinney • *Illustrated by Noryce*

Golda went to visit her friends, Handsome Hank and Tiny Twiz, who live on a farm. She was sure it would be a lot of fun but when she arrived Hank and Twiz looked very sick.

"Hank! Twiz! What's wrong?" asked Golda.

"We ate some of the pigs' slop and now we're sick," chimed the two, very sick puppies. "Could you look after the farm for us this afternoon Golda?" they asked as they dozed off to sleep.

Golda set out to help her friends.   On her way to the barn, she heard a clucking noise from a pen and went to see what it was.

In the pen were a dozen chickens. Some chickens were scratching the dirt and some were sitting on nests.

They paid her no mind until ....

Golda put her nose
under a chicken to see
what it was sitting on!

"CLUCK, CLUCK, squawk, squawk!" the chickens flew into a panic

and pecked Golda right between the eyes with their beaks.

Golda ran out of the chicken coop so fast
that she ran right into the back of a horse.

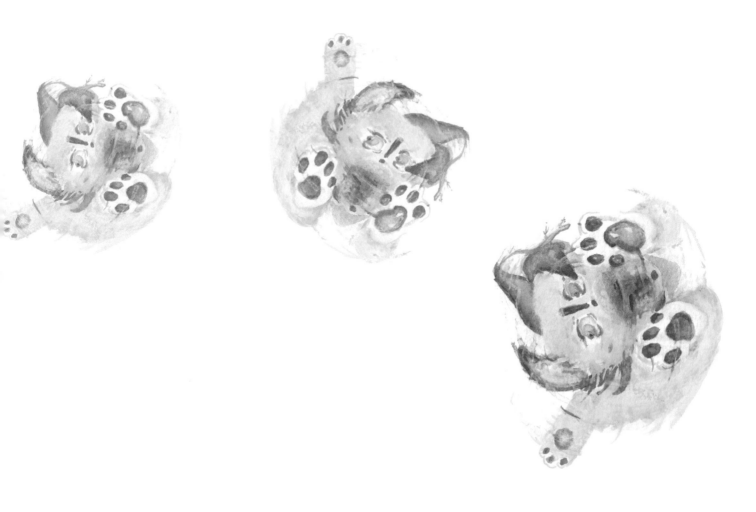

The horse kicked her and head over
heels into the air she went.

She landed right in the middle of a huge mud puddle.

As she stood to shake herself off she saw something move in the mud puddle. It was a pig!

It poked its head up and squealed loudly. It looked like a giant mud monster!

Golda ran as fast as she could away from the pig.

She ran right into a pasture and startled the calves that had been quietly grazing.

Golda followed the calves, as they ran right to their mother. The mother cow stood firmly in place as the calves hid behind her.

Golda bumped right into the mother cow who let out a bellowing "MOOOO!"

Her drool dripped
right down onto
Golda's head.

Golda ducked under the fence to get away from the mother cow, only to find a herd of goats.

The goats were frightened by Golda and began to "BAAA" very loudly.

Quick as a whip, the big Billy Goat came and butted her into the air.

End
over
end

she went right out of the pasture!

Golda landed right in the pond, where
frogs had been sunning on their lily pads.

As she lifted her head, she could see her reflection complete with a bullfrog on the top of her head.

The frog jumped off as Golda
dragged herself out of the pond.

As she shook off, she heard a loud commotion among the
chickens. A fox was trying to sneak into the chicken coop!

Golda sprang into action and chased the fox.
About this time the rooster came around the corner.

The rooster thought Golda had caused the commotion!

He began to flog her with his wings and feet.

The farmer jumped off his tractor to see what the ruckus was all about. He grabbed the rooster, scolded Golda, and sent her back to the house.

Wet, muddy and sore, Golda dragged herself onto the porch where Hank was just waking up from his nap.

"Golda what happened to you?" asked Hank.
"Being a farm dog sure is hard work!" said Golda as
she curled up next to Twiz for a much needed nap.

THE END

Golda Goes to the Farm is the first book in the **Adventures of Golda series**. Follow us at *facebook.com/GoldatheAdventureDog* or check our website at *GoldasAdventures.com* for more information and to find our latest releases.

R. Kinney with Golda the Adventure Dog.

The Adventure of Golda series is born out of a decade of traveling North America. Golda has enjoyed chasing lizards & meeting people from coast to coast. Golda's mom enjoys sharing the awesomeness of discovering nature through writing & photography.

Noryce with Twizzler

Twizzler with her big brown eyes, and playful spirit brings pleasure to my journey. As we hike the forest and mountains, nature fulfills an essence that delights the soul. With this joy, I find my creative spirit.

Made in the USA
San Bernardino, CA
28 February 2018